D1452181

ISBN-13 (Hardcover): 978-1-7356678-0-5
ISBN-13 (Paperback): 978-1-7356678-1-2
ISBN-13 (Digital eBook): 978-1-7356678-2-9

Library of Congress Control Number: 2020923840

Names: Chan, Michelle, author.
Title: My invisible bubble : empowering children to set boundaries / by Michelle Chan.
Description: Temple City, CA : Michelle Chan, 2021. | Summary: This book helps children identify their emotions, pay attention to their comfort levels, express their needs, and set boundaries.
Identifiers: LCCN 2020923840 (print) | ISBN 978-1-7356678-0-5 (hardcover) | ISBN 978-1-7356678-1-2 (paperback) | ISBN 978-1-7356678-2-9 (ebook)
Subjects: LCSH: Picture books for children. | High interest-low vocabulary books. | CYAC: Emotions—Fiction. | Boundaries (Psychology)—Fiction. | Interpersonal relations—Fiction. | BISAC: JUVENILE FICTION / Social Themes / Emotions & Feelings. | JUVENILE FICTION / Social Themes / Self-Esteem & Self-Reliance.
Classification: LCC PZ7.1.C53 My 2021 (print) | LCC PZ7.1.C53 (ebook) | DDC [E]—dc23.

First Edition

Michelle Chan
P.O. Box 237
Temple City, CA 91780

Learn more about Michelle at:
www.MichelleChanLMFT.com

To order additional copies of this book, contact Michelle by email at:
MichelleChanLMFT@gmail.com

Dedicated to the "village" of people who had raised, guided,

taught, supported, and/or unconditionally loved me throughout all these years.

Whether on earth or in heaven, you live forever in my heart!

I have an invisible bubble around me;
It protects me wherever I go.

Even though you can't see it,
It is always there, I know.

The size of my bubble
Shrinks and grows,

Depending on who I'm with
And where I go.

I pay attention to my invisible bubble
And how I feel inside.

It lets me know when I feel safe
Or if I want to run and hide.

When I feel happy and loved, my bubble is small;
I am relaxed and not worried at all.

But when I feel uneasy or scared,
My bubble becomes a big, giant ball.

When people see me all dressed up
And say I am pretty in pink,
They ask if they can give me a hug,
So I take a moment to think...

If I feel comfortable and my bubble is tiny,
I tell them, "It's fine by me!"
If I feel worried and my bubble is huge,
I say, "Thank you, but no," you see.

I have an invisible bubble around me;
It protects me wherever I go.
Even though you can't see it,
It is always there, I know.

When I go to the market with Grandma
And a stranger touches my face,
I feel startled, and my bubble gets bigger,
"Don't touch me," I say.

When I visit Grandpa
And he makes a funny joke,
My invisible bubble dwindles
While I laugh so hard I spit out my Coke.

I have an invisible bubble around me;
It protects me wherever I go.
Even though you can't see it,
It is always there, I know.

When I am at the park with Mommy
And I see my friends playing near,
My invisible bubble deflates
As I run towards them, grinning from ear to ear.

When I go to parties with Daddy
And get picked up by aunties and uncles I don't know,
My invisible bubble swells and my body feels tense,
So I say, "Put me down and let me go."

I have an invisible bubble around me;
It protects me wherever I go.
Even though you can't see it,
It is always there, I know.

When my favorite uncle comes over
To take my brother and me to see a movie,
My invisible bubble is little;
I feel excited and not at all gloomy.

When I'm at school and others make fun of me,
My invisible bubble stretches out wide.
I feel awful and really unhappy,
So I tell them, "That's not all right."

I have an invisible bubble around me;
It protects me wherever I go.
Even though you can't see it,
It is always there, I know.

And did you know?

You have a bubble around you, too!
It protects you wherever you go.
Even though others can't see it,
It is always there, you should know.

If you feel unsafe or uncomfortable,
"Stop it!" you can say.
Talk to an adult you know
And tell them you're not okay.

Even though others can't see your bubble,
It is there to protect you, you know.
So pay attention when your bubble grows and shrinks;
It's telling you more than you think!